A PARRAGON BOOK

Published by
Parragon Books,
Avonbridge Trading Estate,
Avonmouth, Bristol BS11 9QD.

Produced by
Templar Company plc,
don Road, Dorking, Surrey RH4 1JE.

4 Parragon Book Service Limited

ll rights reserved.

by Mark Kingsley-Monks

nd bound in Great Britain

BN 1-85813-635-0

Unit 13-
Atlantic Roa

Th
Pippbrook Mill, I
Copyright © 1

Desigr
Printec

MINI CLASSICS

ALICE IN WONDERLAND

RETOLD BY STEPHANIE LASLETT
ILLUSTRATED BY CAROLE GRAY

||| •PARRAGON• |||

Alice was beginning to get tired of sitting by her sister on the riverbank with nothing to do. She was just wondering whether she should make a daisy chain when a White Rabbit with pink eyes ran by.

"Oh, dear! Oh, dear! I shall be too late!" he exclaimed as he pulled a watch out of his waistcoat pocket. Alice could not believe her eyes. Without a moment's thought, she jumped up and followed the rabbit across the field and was just in time to see him disappear into a hole under the hedge.

She squeezed after him and soon found herself tumbling down a very deep hole. To her surprise, she found herself falling slowly and so had plenty of time to look about her at the shelves and cupboards and pictures as she passed.

"I wonder how many miles I have fallen?" she wondered. "Thousands and thousands, I should think. I must be near the centre of the earth by now!"

Suddenly, with a great thump, she landed on a pile of leaves. In the dark gloom she caught a quick glimpse of the White Rabbit hurrying down a long passage.

"Oh, my ears and whiskers, how late it's getting!" he fussed, as he turned a corner. Quick as a flash, Alice was after him but when she reached the corner he was nowhere to be seen.

Ahead of her was a long, low hall with doors on either side, but when Alice tried the handles they were all locked. A little three-legged glass table stood against one wall and on top was a tiny gold key. But which door would it fit? Then Alice noticed a little door next to the table. The key fitted perfectly and, kneeling down, Alice looked through into the loveliest garden she had ever seen.

"How I wish I was small enough to walk there," sighed

Alice. "But I can't even get my head through the door!" Then she saw something else on top of the table. It was a little bottle with a label saying 'Drink me'. Now Alice was a sensible girl and checked first to see if the bottle was also marked 'Poison'. But there was no other label and when she saw it was safe, Alice drank it all up. It tasted of cherry tart, pineapple, roast turkey and toffee!

"What a curious feeling!" said Alice, for she suddenly realised

that she was growing smaller
and smaller. Soon she was just
the right size to walk through
the door but then she realised
she had left the key on top of
the glass table. Now she was far
too short to reach it! Poor Alice
began to cry with disappointment.
Now she would never be able
to enter the secret garden.

Through her tears, she
caught sight of a tiny glass box
on the floor. Inside was a little
cake with 'Eat me' marked in
currants on the top.

"Maybe this will make me change size, too!" thought Alice. Sure enough, as she swallowed the last crumb, Alice found herself growing taller and taller. "Curiouser and curiouser!" said Alice. "Goodbye, feet!" Now she could unlock the door, but once again she was much too large and walking through was more difficult than ever. Again her tears flowed and soon she was surrounded by a large pool of water.

But what was that? The

pattering of feet could be heard in the distance and, brushing the tears off her cheeks, Alice could see the White Rabbit hurrying towards her.

"Oh! the Duchess, the Duchess!" he wailed. "Oh! won't she be angry if I've kept her waiting!" He was splendidly dressed and carried a pair of white gloves and a fan.

"If you please, sir," said Alice, timidly. The Rabbit jumped with fright, dropped his gloves and fan, and quickly scuttled off.

"Oh, dear," said Alice. "Now I've scared him. Have I changed into someone else? I don't feel like me at all." She tried to remember her school lessons.

"Four times five is twelve, and four times six is thirteen — oh, dear! London is the capital of Paris, and Paris is the capital of Rome — no, that's all wrong!"

Feeling hot and most
peculiar, she picked up the
White Rabbit's fan and tried to
cool herself. Without thinking,
she picked up his tiny gloves
and then saw that she had
managed to pull one of them
over her hand.

"I'm small again!" cried Alice
but, to her dismay, she had once
again left the key on the table.

"Things are worse than ever,"
she sobbed. With a splash! her
foot slipped and she found
herself up to her chin in the

pool of her salty tears. To her
surprise there was a sound of
splashing nearby. It was a little
mouse, swimming to keep afloat.
Soon he was joined by quite a
collection of other curious
creatures and, together, they
all swam for the shore.

They were indeed a queer-
looking party as they gathered
on the bank. With bedraggled
feathers and dripping fur, they
decided that the best thing to
get them dry would be a
Caucus-race.

Alice was very puzzled to discover that the runners in a Caucus-race could begin when they liked and stop when they liked! This meant it was very difficult to decide when the race was over but soon they were all dry once more.

One by one, the small creatures hurried off until Alice was left all alone. Then she spotted the White Rabbit and saw at once that he was upset.

"The Duchess! The Duchess!" he muttered. "Oh, my paws and whiskers. She'll be so angry!" Suddenly he caught sight of Alice. "Mary Ann!" he called. "Run home and fetch me a new pair of gloves and a fan! Quick now!"

"He thinks I'm his maid," laughed Alice as she hurried off.

Soon she came upon a neat little house with 'W. Rabbit' engraved on a bright brass plate. Upstairs she found the gloves and fan but, as she turned to go, her eyes fell on a small bottle.

"Every time I eat or drink, something interesting happens," she thought and, straightaway, drank down half the bottle. What do you think happened next? Yes, Alice began to grow again and in a very short time she had filled the room. One arm stuck out of the window and one foot was jammed up the chimney!

When the White Rabbit arrived he was very cross and stamped up and down the garden path, muttering to

himself. Picking up a handful of pebbles from the path, he tossed them through the window and, to Alice's surprise, they turned into little cakes. As soon as she had swallowed one cake, she began to shrink and in a while was small enough to run outside. She didn't stop to speak but ran as fast as she could into the thick wood.

"I must find something to make me grow big again," she said and there in front of her was a large mushroom.

Sitting on top of the mushroom was a blue caterpillar. He was smoking a pipe called a hookah.

"Who are you?" he asked sleepily, with half-closed eyes.

"I hardly know any more," replied Alice. "I keep growing large, then small and don't keep the same size for ten minutes together!"

"What size do you want to be?" asked the Caterpillar.

"Well, I should like to be a little larger. Three inches is such a wretched size to be."

"It is a very good height indeed!" retorted the Caterpillar, angrily. He reared upright as he spoke and Alice could see he was exactly three inches high!

"Oh, dear!" thought Alice. "Now I've upset him." But as the Caterpillar crawled away he gave Alice some useful information.

"One side will make you grow taller, and the other side will make you grow shorter," he said.

"But which side is which?" wondered Alice, as she broke off two pieces of the mushroom.

She walked on through the wood and soon came upon a little house about four inches high. Coming from the house was the most extraordinary noise; a howling and sneezing and crashing of plates. By nibbling the mushroom she succeeded in making herself the perfect size and, carefully putting the pieces back in her pocket, she walked inside.

There, in the middle of a large smoky kitchen, was the Duchess, sitting on a three-

legged stool and nursing a baby. Behind her was the Cook, busily stirring a large pot of soup. The air was thick with pepper and everyone was sneezing. Lying in front of the fire and grinning from ear to ear was a large cat.

"Why does your cat grin like that?" asked Alice politely.

"It's a Cheshire Cat," replied the Duchess. "Pig!" Alice was shocked to realise that the Duchess was addressing her baby but, taking a deep breath, she decided to ignore this rudery.

"I didn't know that cats could grin," she said, nervously.

"You don't know much," replied the Duchess, "and that's a fact." Alice thought this was most impolite but before she could say anything there was a loud crash. The Cook had begun to throw everything she could reach at the Duchess and her baby.

"Oh, please mind what you're doing!" begged Alice as pots and pans flew through the air.

"Chop off her head!" yelled the Duchess. Then, shaking her baby like a rag doll, she began to sing a lullaby.

"'Speak roughly
to your little boy,
And beat him when he sneezes.
He only does it to annoy,
Because he knows it teases.'
Here! You may nurse it a bit, if you like!" offered the Duchess and she flung the baby at Alice.

"I must go and get ready to play croquet with the Queen."

The baby wriggled so much that Alice nearly dropped him! As she carried him outside into the fresh air, he grunted and Alice looked anxiously at his little face. Once more he grunted and, to her consternation, she saw the baby had a very turned-up nose and very small eyes. There could be no mistake about it. The baby had turned into a pig! Quickly she put him down on the ground and off he trotted into the wood.

Alice felt quite relieved.
"He would have made a
dreadfully ugly child," she
thought, "but now he makes
rather a handsome pig!"

Then she caught sight of the
Cheshire Cat sitting in a tree
and grinning at her.

"Does anyone else live near
here?" asked Alice.

"In that direction," the Cat said, waving her right paw, "lives a Hatter, and in that direction," waving the other paw, "lives a March Hare. Visit either you like: they're both mad." "But I don't want to visit mad people," replied Alice.

"Oh, we're all mad here," said the Cat. "I'm mad. You're mad. You must be mad to have come here."

As Alice considered this, the Cat continued.

"Are you playing croquet with

the Queen today?"

"I haven't been invited yet," replied Alice.

"You'll see me there," said the Cat, and vanished.

By now, Alice was so used to strange things happening that she was not much surprised by this peculiar event. But then the Cat suddenly re-appeared and that gave her quite a shock.

"What became of the baby?" asked the Cat.

"It turned into a pig," replied Alice, rather flustered.

"I do wish you wouldn't keep appearing and vanishing so suddenly. You make me quite giddy," she added

"All right," said the Cat, and this time she vanished quite slowly, beginning with her tail and ending with the grin, which remained there for some time after the rest of her had gone.

"Well, I've often seen a cat without a grin," thought Alice, "But a grin without a cat! It's the most curious thing I ever saw!

Alice set off to visit the March
Hare and soon found his house.
It had ear-shaped chimneys
and a fur-thatched roof. Seated
at a table in the garden were
the March Hare and the Hatter.
Between them, fast asleep, was
a small Dormouse, whom they
leaned on as if he were a
cushion while they talked.

"No room! No room!" they
cried out when they saw Alice.

"There's plenty of room!" she
said indignantly and sat down
in a large armchair.

"Have some wine," said the
March Hare, with a smile.

Alice looked all around the
table but could see nothing
but tea to drink.

"I don't see any wine," she remarked, greatly puzzled.

"There isn't any!" said the March Hare, triumphantly.

"Then it wasn't very polite of you to offer it," said Alice crossly.

"It wasn't very polite of you to sit down without being invited," retorted the March Hare.

"I didn't know it was your table," replied Alice.

The party sat silent for a while and then the Hatter pulled out his watch and shook it next to his ear.

"Two days wrong!" he sighed. "I told you butter wouldn't suit the works," and he glared at the March Hare.

"It was the best butter," the March Hare meekly replied.

"Yes, but some crumbs must have got in there as well," the Hatter grumbled. "You must have put them in with the bread-knife." The March Hare took the watch and looked at it gloomily. Slowly he dipped it into his cup of tea and looked at it again, but he could think of nothing better to say than his first remark,

"It was the *best* butter, you know," he sighed.

"I want a clean cup,"
announced the Hatter. "Let's
all move one place on." They
all moved up which left Alice
sitting in the March Hare's
seat. She wasn't very pleased
because he had spilt milk all
over his plate. Suddenly the
Hatter began to recite.

"Twinkle, twinkle, little bat!
How I wonder what you're at!
Up above the world you fly
Like a tea-tray in the sky.
Twinkle, twinkle...'"
"That's wrong!" thought Alice.

Singing in his sleep, the Dormouse joined in. "Twinkle, twinkle, twinkle, twinkle..." and he carried on for so long that the March Hare and the Hatter had to pinch him to make him stop.

"Tell us a story!" demanded the March Hare, pouring hot water on the Dormouse's nose to wake him up. And so the Dormouse began in a great hurry.

"There were three little sisters and they lived at the bottom of a well and they lived on nothing but treacle..."

"They would have been very ill," interrupted Alice, gently.

"It was a treacle well," continued the Dormouse with a yawn. But he was so tired that he fell fast asleep in the middle of his sentence and never finished the story.

"Well, I don't think..." said Alice.

"Then you shouldn't talk," said the Hatter. This rudeness was more than Alice could bear and off she walked in great disgust.

As she looked back at the tea party she could see the others trying to stuff the sleeping Dormouse into the teapot!

When she turned round again, the first thing Alice saw was a little door right in the middle of a tree trunk. She turned the knob and, to her surprise, found herself back in the long hall with the glass table and the golden key.

"Now I know what to do!" she said, pulling the mushroom from her pocket. She picked up the key and, nibbling away, was soon small enough to walk through the little door and into the beautiful garden with its bright flowerbeds and cool fountains.

Alice was astonished to see three gardeners busily painting white roses with red paint. They were shaped like playing cards and as she got closer she could hear one of them talking.

"Look out now, Five! Don't go splashing paint over me like that!"

"I couldn't help it," said Five in a sulky tone. "Seven jogged my elbow."

Then they noticed Alice.

"The Queen wanted a red rose tree," explained Two, "but we made a mistake and planted a white one. If she finds out, she'll chop off our heads!"

At this moment Five, who had been anxiously looking across the garden, called out to them.

"It's the Queen! The Queen!"
he cried and the three terrified
gardeners instantly threw
themselves flat upon their
faces. There was the sound of
many footsteps and Alice looked
round, eager to see the Queen.

Marching two by two came ten soldiers, then ten courtiers and then, skipping and jumping, the ten royal children. Following them were the guests, including the White Rabbit. Then came the Knave of Hearts, carrying the King's crown on a crimson velvet cushion and, last of all in this grand procession, came THE KING AND QUEEN OF HEARTS.

When they came opposite Alice, the Queen stopped and said severely, "Who is this?"

"My name is Alice, so please your Majesty," replied Alice very politely.

"And who are these?" said the Queen, pointing to the three quaking gardeners.

"How should I know?" said Alice, boldly. "It's certainly no business of mine."

The Queen turned crimson with fury.

"Off with her head!" she screamed, stamping her foot.

"Nonsense!" said Alice, loudly and firmly, and the Queen was

so surprised, she fell silent.
Turning her attention to the
gardeners, she shouted "Get
up!" Up jumped the gardeners
and they began bowing furiously.
When the Queen realised what
they had done to her rose trees,
she glared like a wild beast.

"Off with their heads!" she roared, and the procession moved on.

"Don't worry," whispered Alice, "You shan't be beheaded!" and she popped all three of them inside a large flowerpot until the soldiers had given up their search. As Alice followed the procession, she heard a timid voice at her side.

"It's — it's a very fine day!" said the White Rabbit.

"Very," said Alice, "But where is the Duchess?"

"Hush, hush!" whispered the Rabbit nervously. "She's under sentence of execution for boxing the Queen's ears!" Alice burst out laughing but was interrupted by the Queen shouting in a voice like thunder.

"Get to your places!"

The croquet game was about to begin and people began running about in all directions as they scrambled to find their positions. When Alice saw the croquet ground she could hardly believe her eyes.

The balls were curled-up hedgehogs, the mallets were flamingos and the soldiers had to bend over and touch the ground to make the arches. Alice found the game very difficult. By the time she had tucked her flamingo under her arm, straightened out his neck and was ready to play, the hedgehog 'ball' had crawled away! The players quarrelled and fought with each other and the Queen stamped about shouting "Off with their heads!"

Alice was wondering how she could get away without being seen when she saw something peculiar in the air. It puzzled her very much at first but then she saw it was a grin and soon the Cheshire Cat appeared.

"How are you getting on?" asked the Cat.

"It's all very confusing," admitted Alice.

The King saw her speaking to the Cat. "Who are you talking to?" he asked. "I don't like the look of that animal at all."

"Off with her head!" shouted the Queen, glaring at the Cat.

Alice thought she better continue with the game but was annoyed to find that her hedgehog was now involved in a fight and her flamingo was trying to fly up into a tree.

Soon everyone, apart from the King, the Queen and Alice, was under sentence of execution

and had been carried away by the soldiers. The Queen turned to Alice.

"It's time you met the Mock Turtle," she said. Soon they came upon a Gryphon, lying fast asleep in the sun.

"Up, lazy thing!" ordered the Queen, "and take this young lady to meet the Mock Turtle. I have some executions to watch."

As they watched the Queen walk away, the Gryphon chuckled. "They never execute anyone, you know. It's just her fancy."

They had not gone far before they saw the Mock Turtle in the distance, sitting sad and lonely on a little ledge of rock. As they came nearer, Alice could hear him sighing as if his heart would break. She felt very sorry for him.

"Why is he so sad?" she asked the Gryphon. With large eyes brim full of tears, the Mock Turtle looked at Alice.

"I'll tell you," he said in a deep, hollow tone. After several deep sighs he carried on. "I was once a real Turtle. I went to a school in the sea. The master was an old Turtle — we used to call him Tortoise — "

"Why did you call him Tortoise, if he wasn't one?" Alice asked.

"Because he taught us," said the Mock Turtle, angrily.

"We studied Mystery, ancient
and modern, with Seaography;
then Drawling — the Drawling-
master was an old conger-eel
and used to come once a week.
He taught us Drawling, Stretching
and Fainting in Coils."

"And how many hours a day
did you do lessons?" asked Alice.

"Ten hours the first day," said
the Mock Turtle, "nine the next,
and so on."

"What a curious plan!"
exclaimed Alice. "That's the
reason they're called lessons,"

the Gryphon remarked, "because they lessen from day to day."

This was quite a new idea to Alice, and she thought it over a little before she made her next remark. "Then the eleventh day must have been a holiday?"

"Of course it was," said the Mock Turtle. He sighed deeply and drew the back of one flapper across his eyes. With tears running down his cheeks he went on.

"Do you know a dance called the Lobster Quadrille?" he asked.

When Alice admitted she did not know this particular dance, the Mock Turtle and the old Gryphon slowly got up and demonstrated. They danced very solemnly around Alice, every now and then treading on her toes when they passed too close. In a slow, sad voice the Mock Turtle began to sing. "'Will you walk a little faster?' said a whiting to a snail. 'There's a porpoise close behind us, and he's treading on my tail.'"

"Boots and shoes under the sea," said the Gryphon, "are polished with whiting."

"And what are they made of?" asked Alice, full of curiosity.

"Soles and eels, of course," the Gryphon replied rather impatiently. "Any shrimp could have told you that."

The Mock Turtle began another song but, before he could finish, Alice heard a far-off cry.

"The trial's beginning!"

"Come on!" cried the Gryphon,

and, pulling Alice by the hand, he hurried off.

The Court of Justice was packed full of excited birds and animals. Seated on their thrones at one end of the room were the King and Queen of Hearts, looking very grand.

Standing in front of them, bound in chains, was their son, the Knave of Hearts and on a table in the centre of the room, was a large plate of tarts.

"I wish they'd hand them round!" thought Alice.

Next to the King stood the
White Rabbit with a trumpet
in one hand and a scroll of
parchment in the other.

"Silence in court" he cried.

Gradually the twittering and chattering died down and all was quiet in the courtroom.

"Herald, read the accusation!" ordered the King.

The White Rabbit blew three blasts on the trumpet, then unrolled the parchment scroll, and read as follows:

"'The Queen of Hearts,
She made some tarts,
All on a summer's day.
The Knave of Hearts,
He stole those tarts,
And took them clean away!'"

The King called for the first
witness and in came the Hatter.
He held a teacup in one hand
and a piece of bread and butter
in the other. Following him,
arm in arm, were the March
Hare and the Dormouse. The
poor Hatter was so nervous
that he took a large bite out of
his teacup by mistake!

Just at this moment Alice felt
a very curious sensation.

"I wish you wouldn't squeeze
so," complained the Dormouse.

"I can't help it," apologised

Alice. "I'm growing again!"

"Call the next witness," cried out the King and, to Alice's surprise, she heard her own name being shouted by the White Rabbit.

"Here!" she cried, quite forgetting how large she had grown. Jumping up, she tipped the jurybox over and knocked the jurors sprawling into the protesting crowd.

"Silence!" cried the King. "Rule 42. All persons more than a mile high must leave the court."

Alice thought this was quite ridiculous.

"Stuff and nonsense!" she said loudly. Everyone turned and stared at her

"Hold your tongue!" said the Queen, turning purple.

"I won't!" declared Alice.

"Off with her head!" screamed the Queen at the top of her voice. Nobody moved.

"Who cares for you?" said Alice, who had grown to her full size by this time. "You're nothing but a pack of cards!"

At this, the whole pack rose up into the air and came flying down upon her. Alice gave a little scream, half of fright and half of anger, and tried to beat them off — and found herself lying on the riverbank, with her head in her sister's lap. Her sister gently brushed away some leaves which had fluttered down upon Alice's face.

"Wake up, Alice dear!" she said. "Why, what a long sleep you've had!"

Then Alice, with shining eyes, and a simple and loving heart, described her curious dream and her big sister, half-believing in this Wonderland, could almost hear the soft pattering of the White Rabbit's feet.

LEWIS CARROLL

Alice's Adventures in Wonderland, first published in 1865, was written by Charles Dodgson (1832-1898) under his pen-name, Lewis Carroll. The story grew out of his friendship with young Alice Liddell, one of many children who were frequently entertained by his wonderful storytelling. After a picnic shared with Alice and her sisters ended in a downpour of rain, Charles Dodgson decided to begin a new story and "sent my heroine straight down a rabbit-hole … without the least idea what was to happen afterwards". Little Alice begged him to write down the story and so *Alice's Adventures in Wonderland* took its first step towards the worldwide reputation it enjoys today. By the time of his death, it was the most popular children's book in England, and by the time of his centenary in 1932, one of the most famous in all the world.